ЯWAЯ∂T∂

PEDRO

PEDRO'S BIG
GOAL

WITHDRAWN

by Fran Manushkin

illustrated by
Tammie Lyon

PICTURE WINDOW BOOKS
a capstone imprint

Pedro is published by Picture Window Books,
a Capstone Imprint
1710 Roe Crest Drive
North Mankato, Minnesota 56003
www.mycapstone.com

Text © 2017 Fran Manushkin
Illustrations © 2017 Picture Window Books

All rights reserved. No part of this publication may be reproduced in whole or in
part, or stored in a retrieval system, or transmitted in any form or by any means,
electronic, mechanical, photocopying, recording, or otherwise, without written
permission of the publisher.

Library of Congress Cataloging-in-Publication Data

Names: Manushkin, Fran, author. | Lyon, Tammie, illustrator.
Title: Pedro's big goal / by Fran Manushkin; [illustrator, Tammie Lyon].
Description: North Mankato, Minnesota: Picture Window Books, a Capstone
    imprint, 2016. | ?2017 | Series: Pedro | Summary: Pedro would love to be
    the goalie in the team's first game, but another boy is bigger—so all his friends
    come over to help him practice before the tryout.
Identifiers: LCCN 2015046882| ISBN 9781515800866 (library binding) | ISBN
    9781515800903 (pbk.) | ISBN 9781515800941 (ebook (pdf))
Subjects: LCSH: Hispanic Americans—Juvenile fiction. | Soccer goalkeepers—
    Juvenile fiction. | Teamwork (Sports)—Juvenile fiction. Friendship—Juvenile
    fiction. | CYAC: Hispanic Americans—Fiction. | Soccer—Fiction. | Teamwork
    (Sports)—Fiction. | Friendship—Fiction.
Classification: LCC PZ7.M3195 Pci 2016 | DDC 813.54—dc23
LC record available at http://lccn.loc.gov/2015046882

Designers: Aruna Rangarajan and Tracy McCabe
Design Elements: Shutterstock

Photo Credits:
Greg Holch, pg. 26
Tammie Lyon, pg. 26

Printed and bound in China.
010119R

Table of Contents

Chapter 1
Goalie Tryouts

Pedro didn't like soccer.

He LOVED soccer. He loved

running and kicking and

jumping.

"Our team is the best!"

he bragged. "Hurray for the

Jumping Wildcats."

Katie Woo cheered too.

"We run fast. We jump high.

We kick hard!"

Coach Rush said, "Next
week, I'm picking a goalie for
our first game. Who wants to
try out?"

"Me! Me! Me!" yelled

everyone.

"Forget it!" sneered Roddy.

"I'm the biggest. Nobody can

beat me."

"Roddy's right," said Pedro.

"He will be the best."

"I'm not so sure," said

Katie. "Bigger is not always

better."

Katie and JoJo and Barry went home with Pedro to practice.

Katie kicked the ball to Pedro.

WHOOSH! It went past him.

"Try again!" yelled Barry.

He kicked the ball to Pedro.

WHOOSH! Pedro missed again.

Chapter 2
Practice and Poop

Pedro told his dad, "Maybe I can't move fast enough to be a goalie."

"Don't give up!" said his dad.

"Okay," agreed Pedro. "I'll keep trying."

"I want to play too," said

Pedro's brother, Paco.

"Watch out!" Pedro yelled.

He blocked Paco from

jumping into a pile of puppy

poop.

"Good block!" said Pedro's dad.

He kicked the ball to Pedro. Pedro almost blocked it.

"Keep trying," said his dad. "You will get better."

The next day, Pedro's

friends came over to play.

Barry kicked the ball.

Oops! He kicked it too

hard, and the ball flew over

the fence.

"Arf!" Pedro's puppy, Peppy, chased the ball. He tried to jump over the fence and into the street!

Pedro jumped high. He

blocked Peppy!

"Wow!" cheered Barry. "That

was the best block of all."

"I'll say!" Pedro smiled,

hugging Peppy tight.

Pedro kept on

practicing.

"I wonder who

the coach will

pick to be goalie?"

asked Katie.

"Maybe it

will be Roddy,"

said JoJo.

"Maybe not,"

said Barry.

Chapter 3
The Wildcats' Goalie

Finally, the day came for

the tryouts. Katie went first.

She missed both balls.

"Better luck next time,"

said Coach Rush.

Then it was JoJo's turn.

She blocked one ball, but she

missed the next one.

"Not bad," said Coach

Rush. "Let's see who can block

both balls."

"It's my turn," yelled Roddy.

"I know I will win."

But Roddy was so busy

bragging he missed both balls.

Then it was Pedro's turn.

Roddy kicked the first ball.

Pedro blocked it!

Roddy kicked the second

ball. Pedro jumped.

He blocked that one too!

"You win!" yelled Coach Rush. "Pedro is our goalie."

"Yay!" cheered Pedro's friends. "We knew you could do it."

"Now I know too," said Pedro. "I get a big kick out of this game."

He smiled all the way home.

About the Author

Fran Manushkin is the author of many popular picture books, including *Happy in Our Skin*; *Baby, Come Out!*; *Latkes and Applesauce: A Hanukkah Story*; *The Tushy Book*; *The Belly Book*; and *Big Girl Panties*. Fran writes on her beloved Mac computer in New York City, without the help of her two naughty cats, Chaim and Goldy.

About the Illustrator

Tammie Lyon began her love for drawing at a young age while sitting at the kitchen table with her dad. She continued her love of art and eventually attended the Columbus College of Art and Design, where she earned a bachelor's degree in fine art. After a brief career as a professional ballet dancer, she decided to devote herself full-time to illustration. Today she lives with her husband, Lee, in Cincinnati, Ohio. Her dogs, Gus and Dudley, keep her company as she works in her studio.

Glossary

bragged (BRAGD)—talked about how good you are at something

cheered (CHIHRD)—shouted encouragement or approval

goalie (GOH-lee)—someone who guards the goal in soccer to keep the other team from scoring

sneered (SNIHRD)—smiled in a hateful or rude way

tryout (TRY-out)—a test to see if a person is able to do something such as play on a team

Let's Talk

1. Pedro loves soccer. What is your favorite sport? What do you like about it?

2. Pedro practiced a lot to get ready for the goalie tryouts. Why is it important to practice? How would the story have been different if he hadn't practiced?

3. Roddy said no one could beat him and he was going to be the best. How do you think that made Pedro feel?

Let's Write

1. Pedro's parents and friends helped him practice to be a goalie. Write about a time you helped a friend.

2. Pedro's soccer team name is the Jumping Wildcats. Write down the names of your favorite sports teams.

3. Draw a picture of yourself playing your favorite sport. Write a paragraph about why you like it.

JOKE AROUND

Why do soccer players get good grades?
They're always using their heads!

What do you call a soccer player made of swiss cheese?
a holey goalie

What did one soccer shoe say to the other?
"Between us, we're gonna have a ball!"

Why is a soccer stadium the coolest place in the world?
Because it's full of fans.

⚽ What did the bumble bee say when it kicked the soccer ball?
"Hive scored!"

⚽ Why did the soccer ball quit the team?
It was tired of getting kicked around.

⚽ Why was Cinderella thrown off the soccer team?
Because she ran away from the ball.

THE FUN DOESN'T STOP HERE!

Discover more at www.capstonekids.com

- ⚽ Videos & Contests
- ⚽ Games & Puzzles
- ⚽ Friends & Favorites
- ⚽ Authors & Illustrators

Find cool websites and more books like this one at www.facthound.com. Just type in the Book ID: 9781515800866 and you're ready to go!

31901060285428